D1162688

HAVERHILL
PUBLIC LIBRARY

This item was purchased with
funds from private donors to
maintain the collection of the
Haverhill Public Library.

IDW

JOHNSON
MOLNAR

STAR TRE

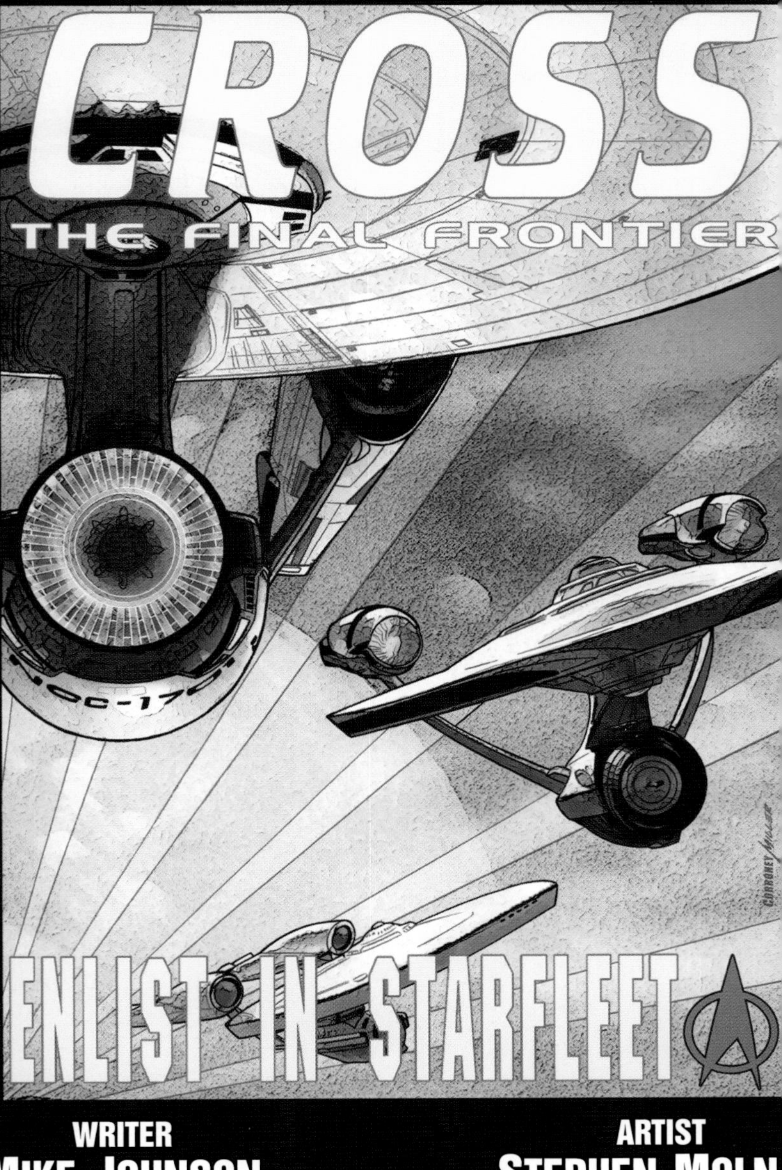

CROSS
THE FINAL FRONTIER
NCC-170
ENLIST IN STARFLEET

WRITER
MIKE JOHNSON

ARTIST
STEPHEN MOLN

COLORIST
JOHN RAUCH

LETTERER
NEIL UYETAKE

BASED ON THE ORIGINAL TELEPLAY OF *WHERE NO MAN HAS GONE BE*
SAMUEL A. PEEPLES

CREATIVE CONSULTANT
ROBERTO ORCI

EDITOR
SCOTT DUNBIE

Visit us at www.abdopublishing.com

Reinforced library bound editions published in 2014 by Spotlight, a division of the ABDO Group, PO Box 398166, Minneapolis, MN 55439. Spotlight produces high-quality reinforced library bound editions for schools and libraries. Published by agreement with IDW.

Printed in the United States of America, North Mankato, Minnesota.
042013
092013
♻ This book contains at least 10% recycled material.

STAR TREK created by Gene Roddenberry.
Special thanks to Risa Kessler and John Van Citters of CBS Consumer Products for their invaluable assistance.

STAR TREK: Where No Man Has Gone Before: Part 1. ® & © 2011 CBS Studios Inc. *STAR TREK* and related marks and trademarks of CBS Studios Inc. © 2011 Paramount Pictures Corporation. All Rights Reserved. IDW Publishing authorized user. © 2011 Idea and Design Works, LLC. IDW Publishing, a division of Idea and Design Works, LLC. Any similarites to persons living or dead are purely coincidental. With the exception of artwork used for review purposes, none of the contents of this publication may be reprinted without the permission of Idea and Design Works, LLC.

Library of Congress Cataloging-in-Publication Data

Johnson, Mike.
  Where no man has gone before / story by Mike Johnson ; art by Stephen Molnar.
    volumes cm. -- (Star Trek)
  ISBN 978-1-61479-161-4 (part 1) -- ISBN 978-1-61479-162-1 (part 2)
1. Graphic novels. I. Molnar, Stephen, illustrator. II. Title.
  PZ7.7.J6417Whe 2014
  741.5'973--dc23
                            2013004267

All Spotlight books are reinforced library bindings
and manufactured in the United States of America.

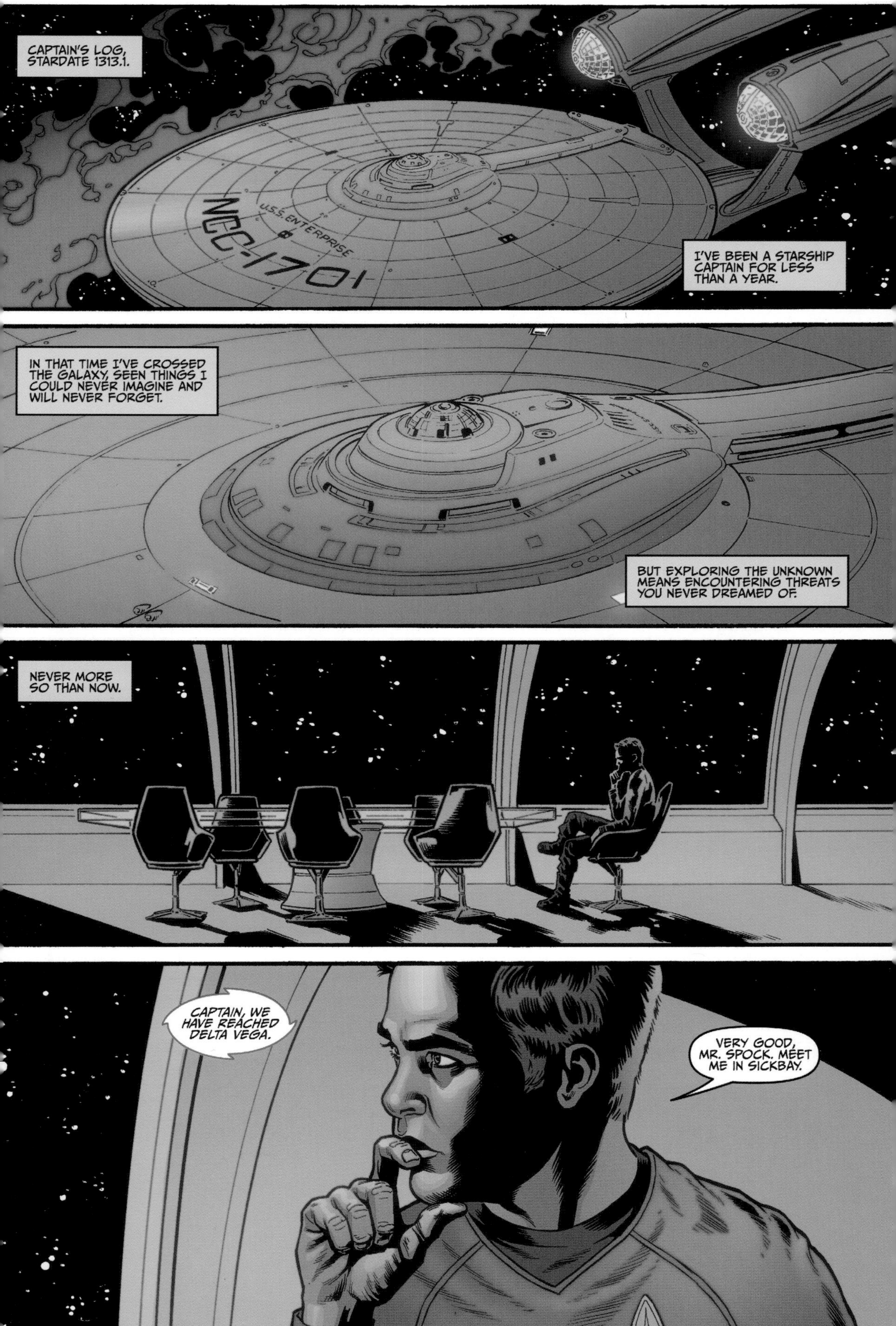
CAPTAIN'S LOG, STARDATE 1313.1.
NCC-1701
U.S.S. ENTERPRISE
I'VE BEEN A STARSHIP CAPTAIN FOR LESS THAN A YEAR.
IN THAT TIME I'VE CROSSED THE GALAXY, SEEN THINGS I COULD NEVER IMAGINE AND WILL NEVER FORGET.
BUT EXPLORING THE UNKNOWN MEANS ENCOUNTERING THREATS YOU NEVER DREAMED OF.
NEVER MORE SO THAN NOW.
CAPTAIN, WE HAVE REACHED DELTA VEGA.
VERY GOOD, MR. SPOCK. MEET ME IN SICKBAY.

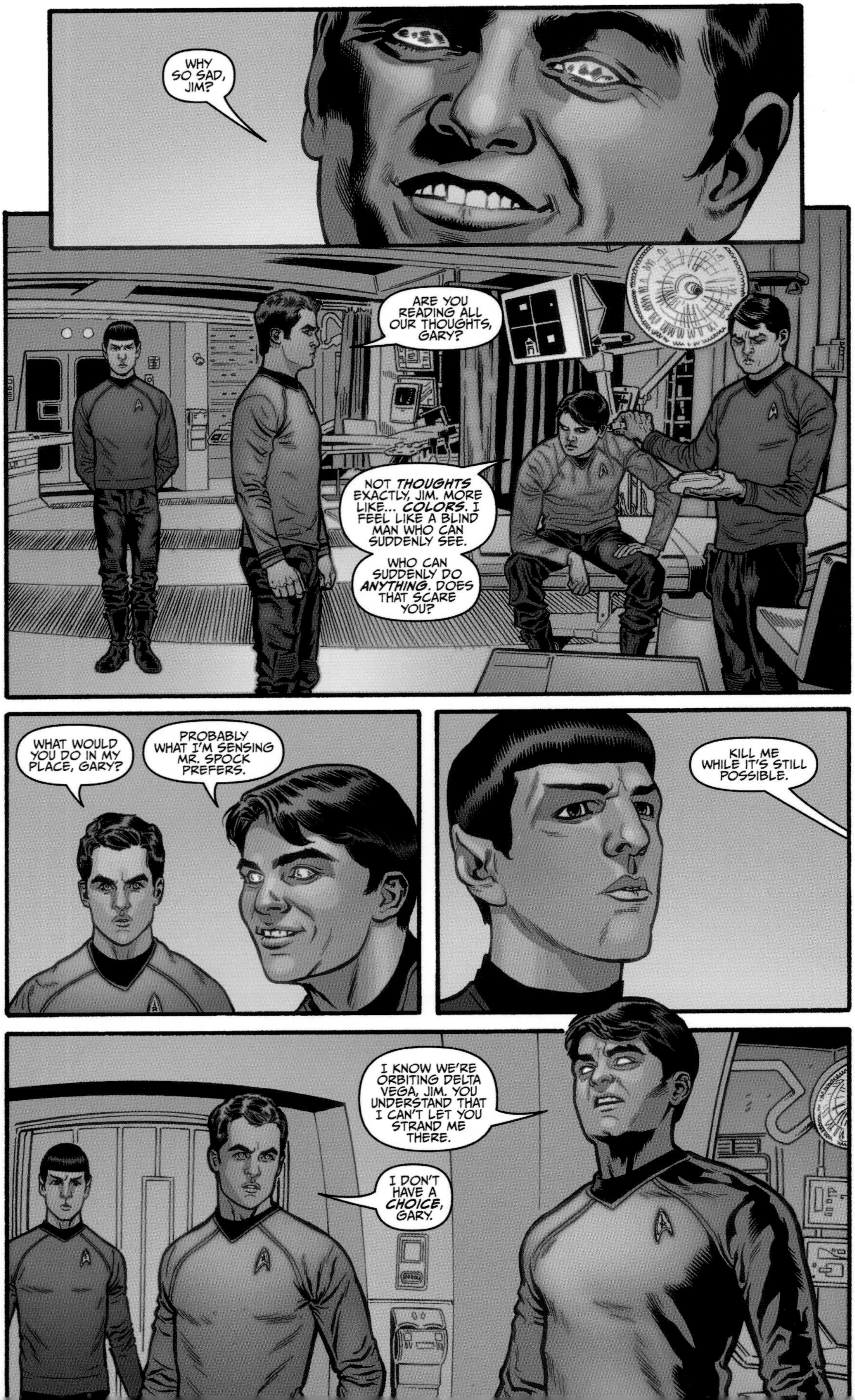
WHY SO SAD, JIM?
ARE YOU READING ALL OUR THOUGHTS, GARY?
NOT *THOUGHTS* EXACTLY, JIM. MORE LIKE... *COLORS.* I FEEL LIKE A BLIND MAN WHO CAN SUDDENLY SEE.
WHO CAN SUDDENLY DO *ANYTHING*. DOES THAT SCARE YOU?
WHAT WOULD YOU DO IN MY PLACE, GARY?
PROBABLY WHAT I'M SENSING MR. SPOCK PREFERS.
KILL ME WHILE IT'S STILL POSSIBLE.
I KNOW WE'RE ORBITING DELTA VEGA, JIM. YOU UNDERSTAND THAT I CAN'T LET YOU STRAND ME THERE.
I DON'T HAVE A *CHOICE*, GARY.

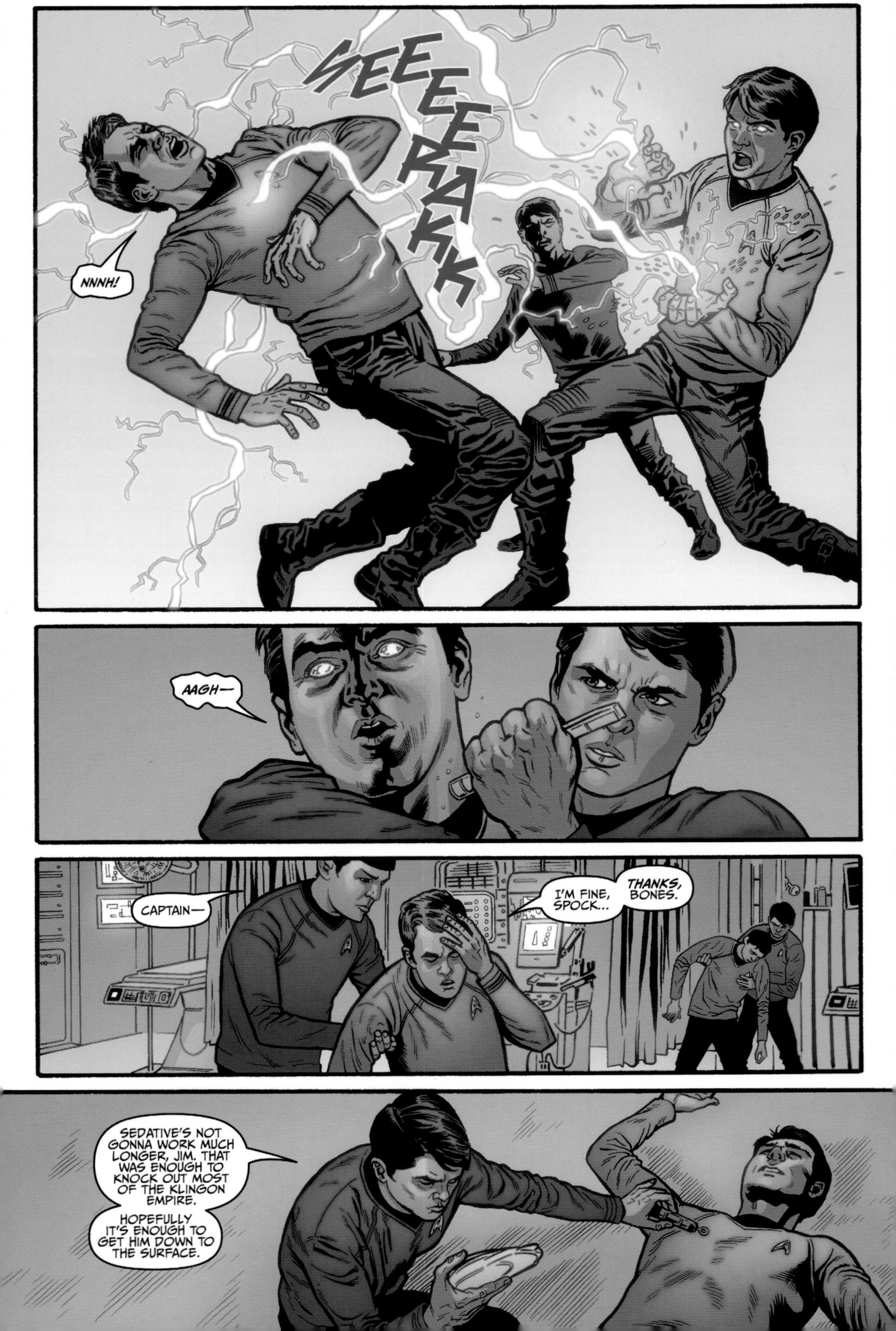
SEEEERAKK
NNNH!
AAGH—
CAPTAIN—
I'M FINE, SPOCK...
THANKS, BONES.
SEDATIVE'S NOT GONNA WORK MUCH LONGER, JIM. THAT WAS ENOUGH TO KNOCK OUT MOST OF THE KLINGON EMPIRE.
HOPEFULLY IT'S ENOUGH TO GET HIM DOWN TO THE SURFACE.

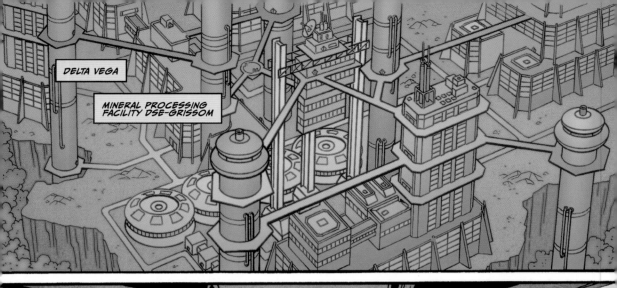

DELTA VEGA

MINERAL PROCESSING FACILITY DSE-GRISSOM

VVVZZZHHNN

MR. SCOTT, YOU AND KELSO FIND WHAT YOU NEED TO GET WARP BACK ONLINE. I DON'T WANT TO STAY HERE A SECOND LONGER THAN WE NEED TO.

AYE, SIR!

SPOCK, WE'LL PUT GARY IN THE STATION'S CREW QUARTERS. GET THE FORCE FIELD READY. AS SOON AS HE'S SECURE...

...WE'RE GONE.

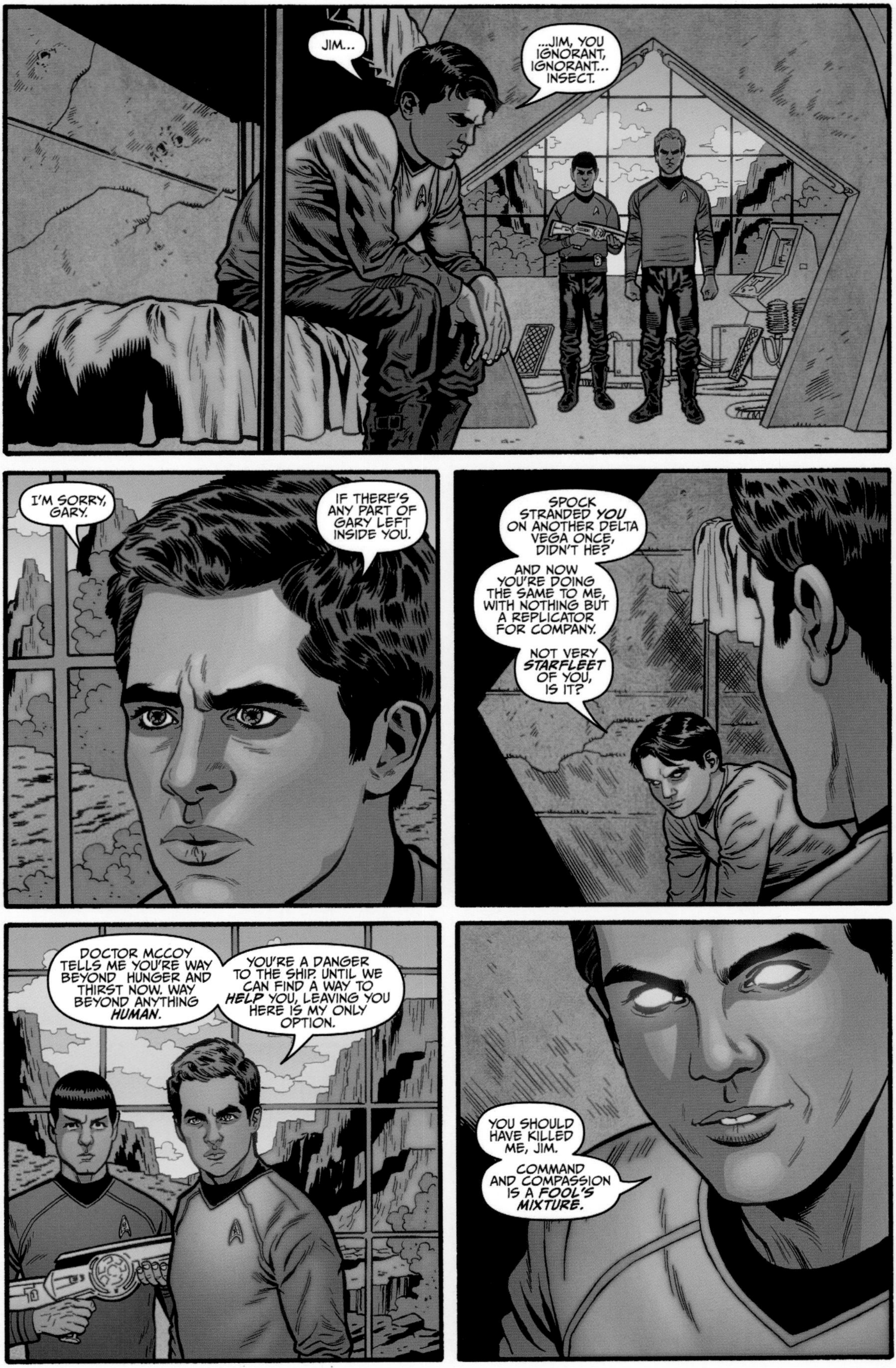
JIM...
...JIM, YOU IGNORANT, IGNORANT... INSECT.
I'M SORRY, GARY.
IF THERE'S ANY PART OF GARY LEFT INSIDE YOU.
SPOCK STRANDED *YOU* ON ANOTHER DELTA VEGA ONCE, DIDN'T HE?
AND NOW YOU'RE DOING THE SAME TO ME, WITH NOTHING BUT A REPLICATOR FOR COMPANY.
NOT VERY *STARFLEET* OF YOU, IS IT?
DOCTOR MCCOY TELLS ME YOU'RE WAY BEYOND HUNGER AND THIRST NOW. WAY BEYOND ANYTHING *HUMAN*.
YOU'RE A DANGER TO THE SHIP. UNTIL WE CAN FIND A WAY TO *HELP* YOU, LEAVING YOU HERE IS MY ONLY OPTION.
YOU SHOULD HAVE KILLED ME, JIM.
COMMAND AND COMPASSION IS A *FOOL'S MIXTURE*.

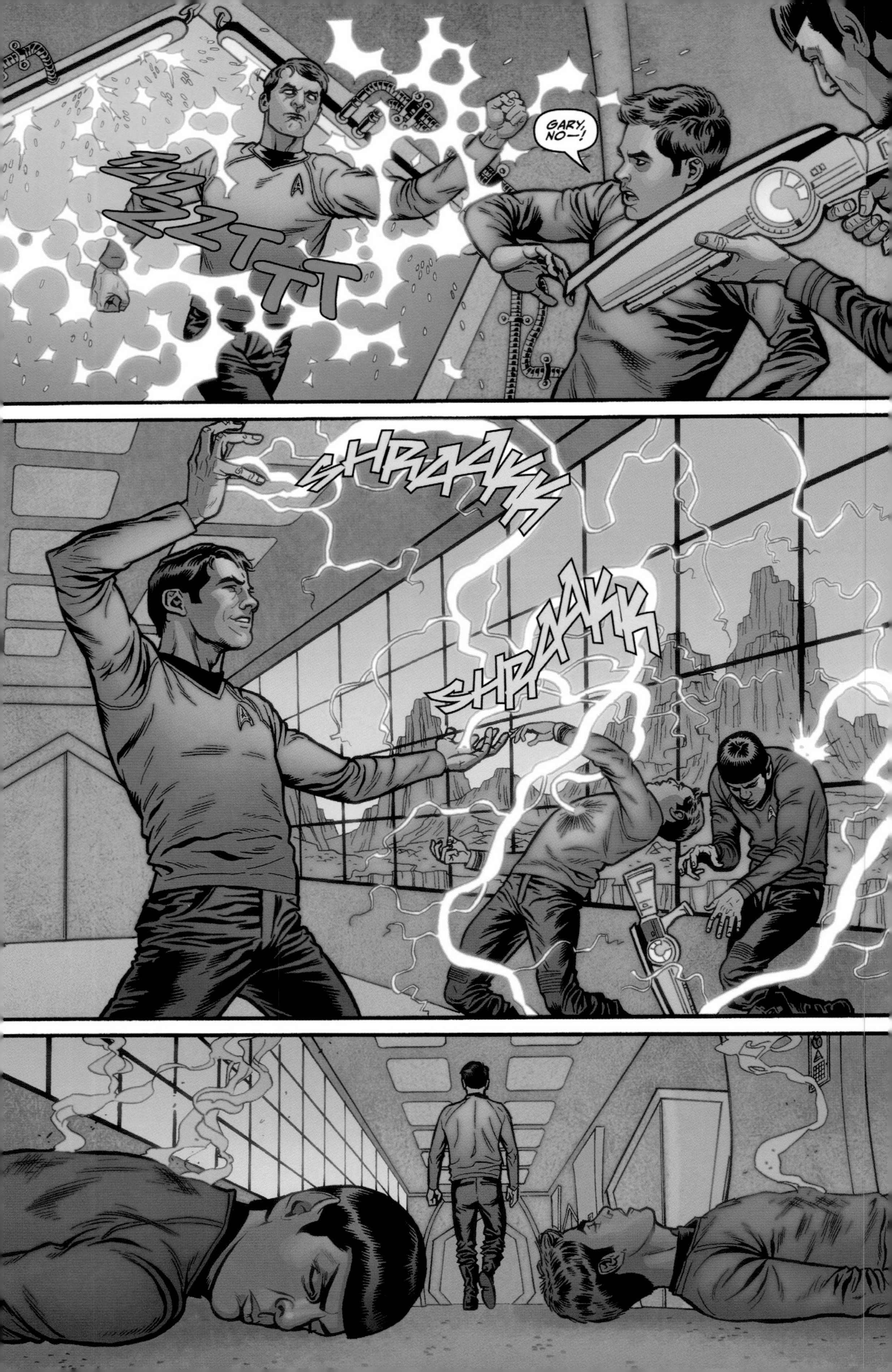
ZZZTTT
GARY, NO—!
SHRAAKK
SHRAAKK

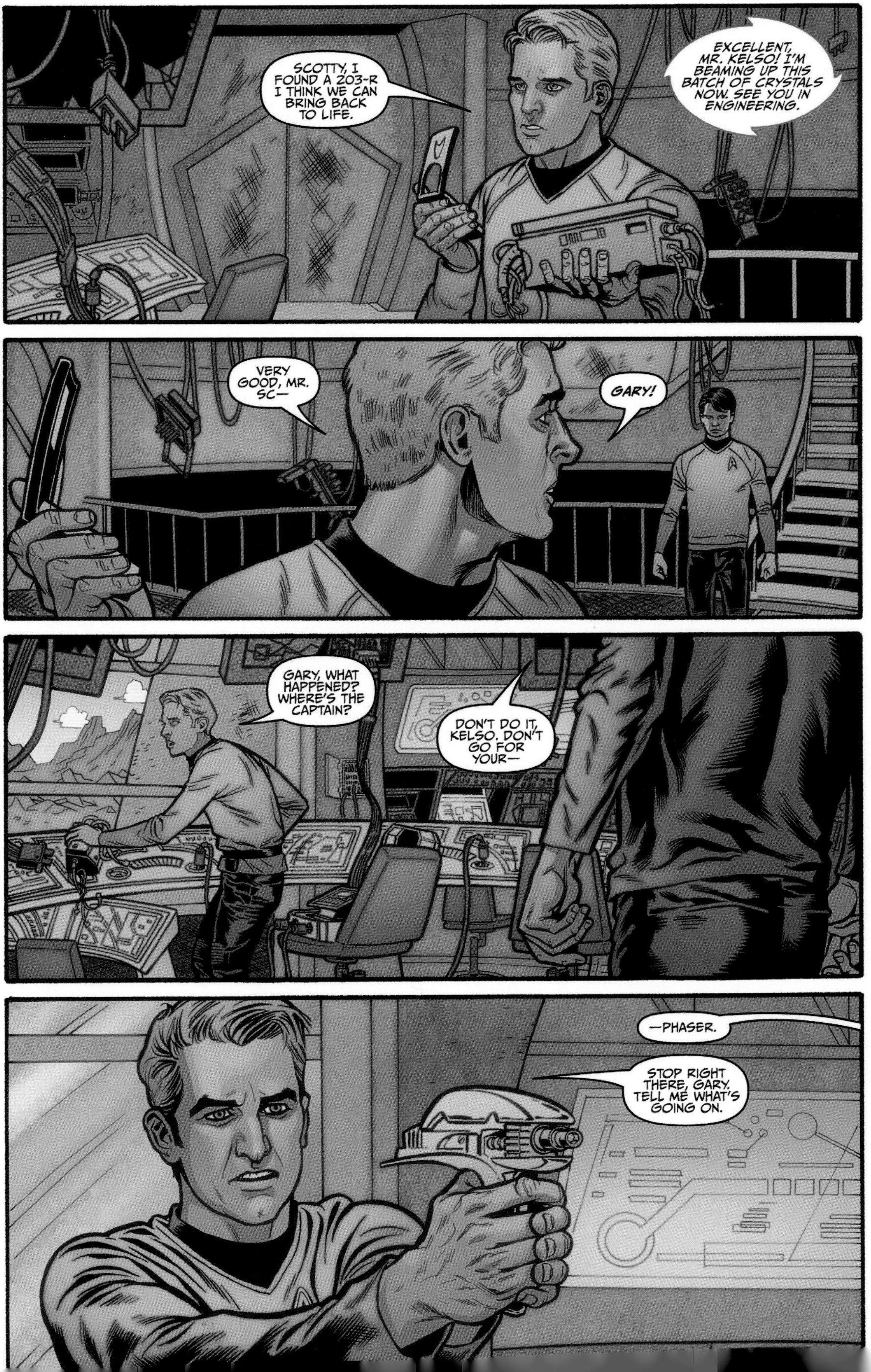
SCOTTY, I FOUND A 203-R I THINK WE CAN BRING BACK TO LIFE.
EXCELLENT, MR. KELSO! I'M BEAMING UP THIS BATCH OF CRYSTALS NOW. SEE YOU IN ENGINEERING.
VERY GOOD, MR. SC—
GARY!
GARY, WHAT HAPPENED? WHERE'S THE CAPTAIN?
DON'T DO IT, KELSO. DON'T GO FOR YOUR—
—PHASER.
STOP RIGHT THERE, GARY. TELL ME WHAT'S GOING ON.

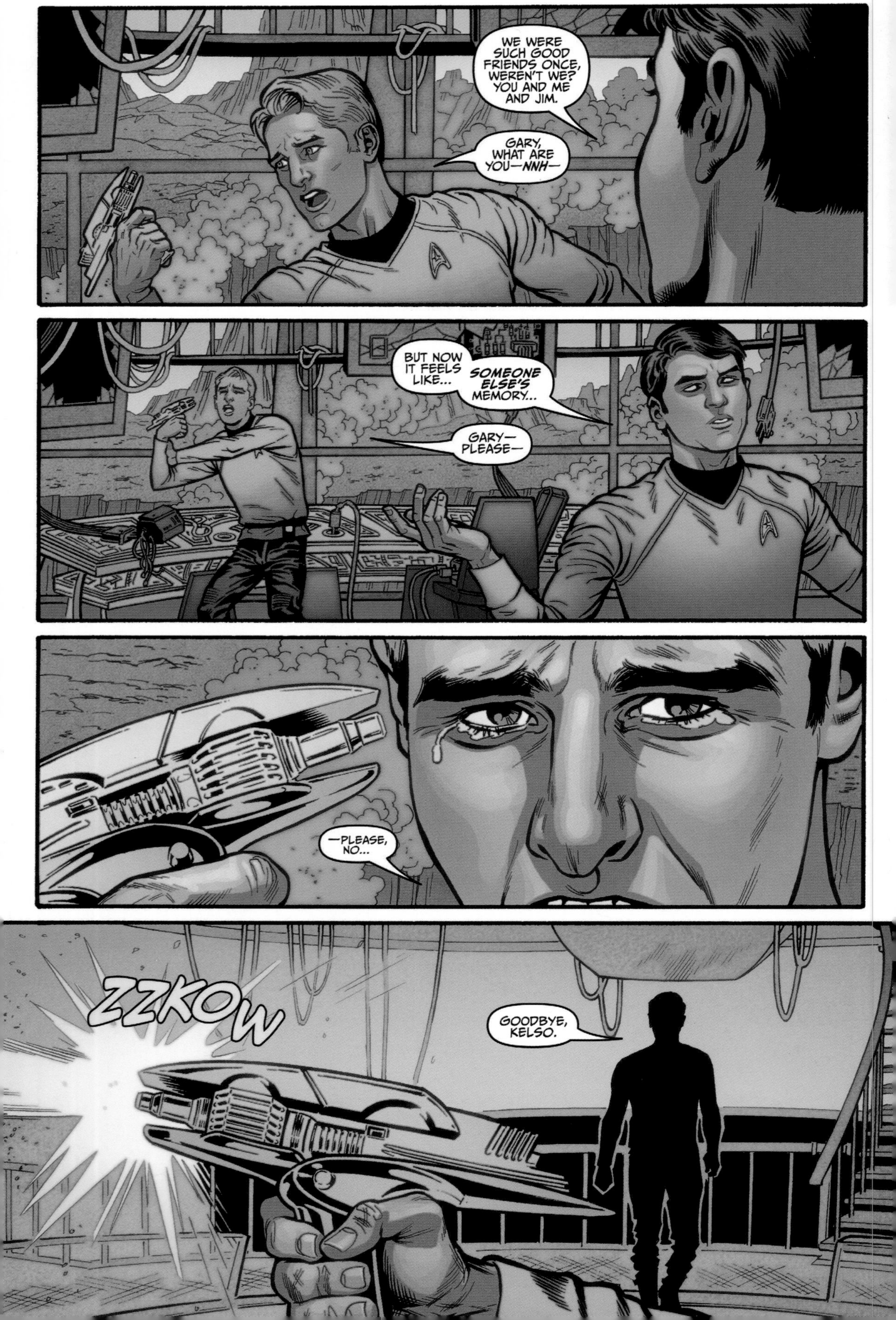
WE WERE SUCH GOOD FRIENDS ONCE, WEREN'T WE? YOU AND ME AND JIM.
GARY, WHAT ARE YOU—*NNH*—
BUT NOW IT FEELS LIKE...
SOMEONE ELSE'S MEMORY...
GARY—PLEASE—
—PLEASE, NO...
ZZKOW
GOODBYE, KELSO.

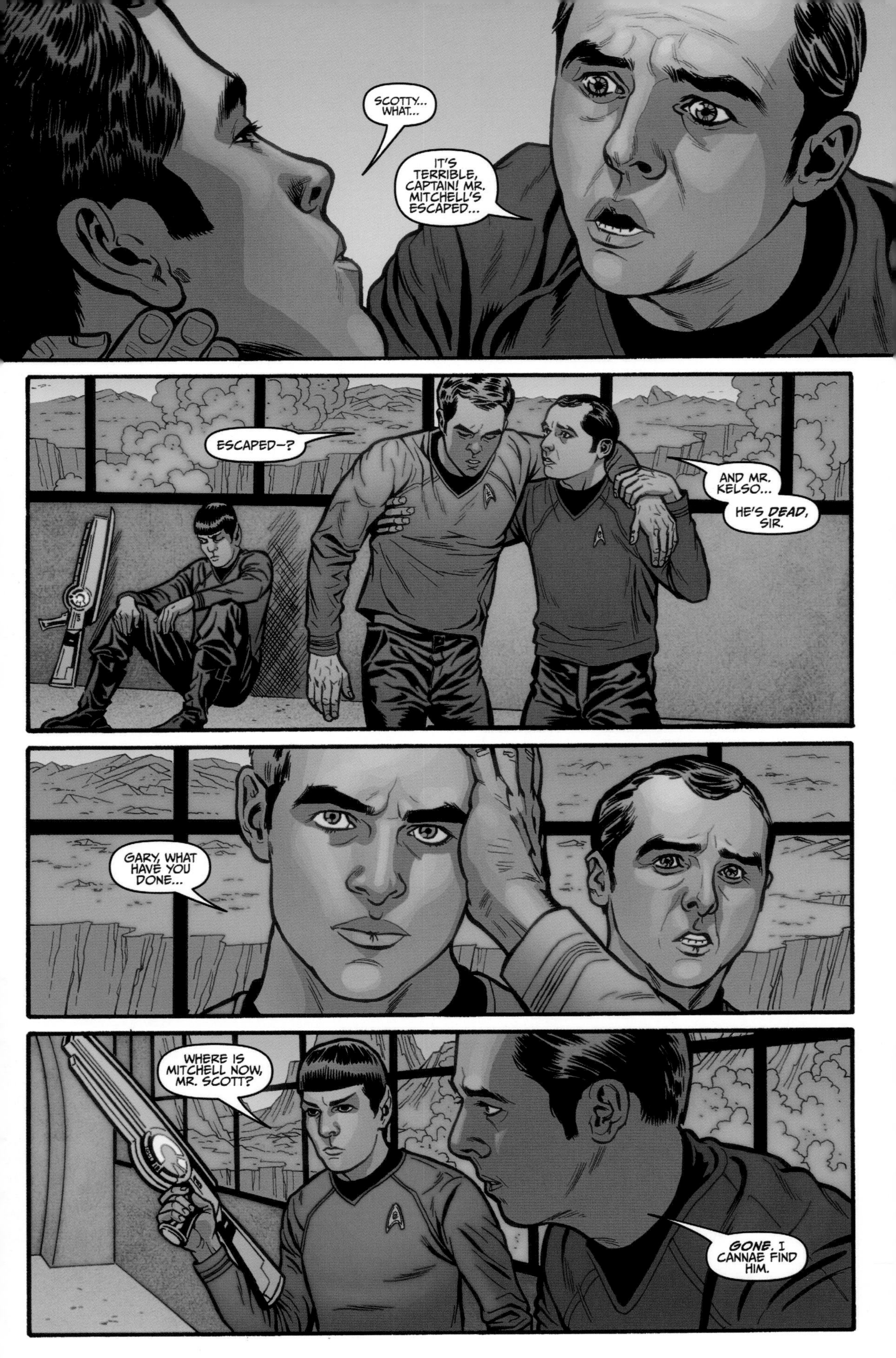
SCOTTY... WHAT...
IT'S TERRIBLE, CAPTAIN! MR. MITCHELL'S ESCAPED...
ESCAPED--?
AND MR. KELSO...
HE'S *DEAD*, SIR.
GARY, WHAT HAVE YOU DONE...
WHERE IS MITCHELL NOW, MR. SCOTT?
GONE. I CANNAE FIND HIM.

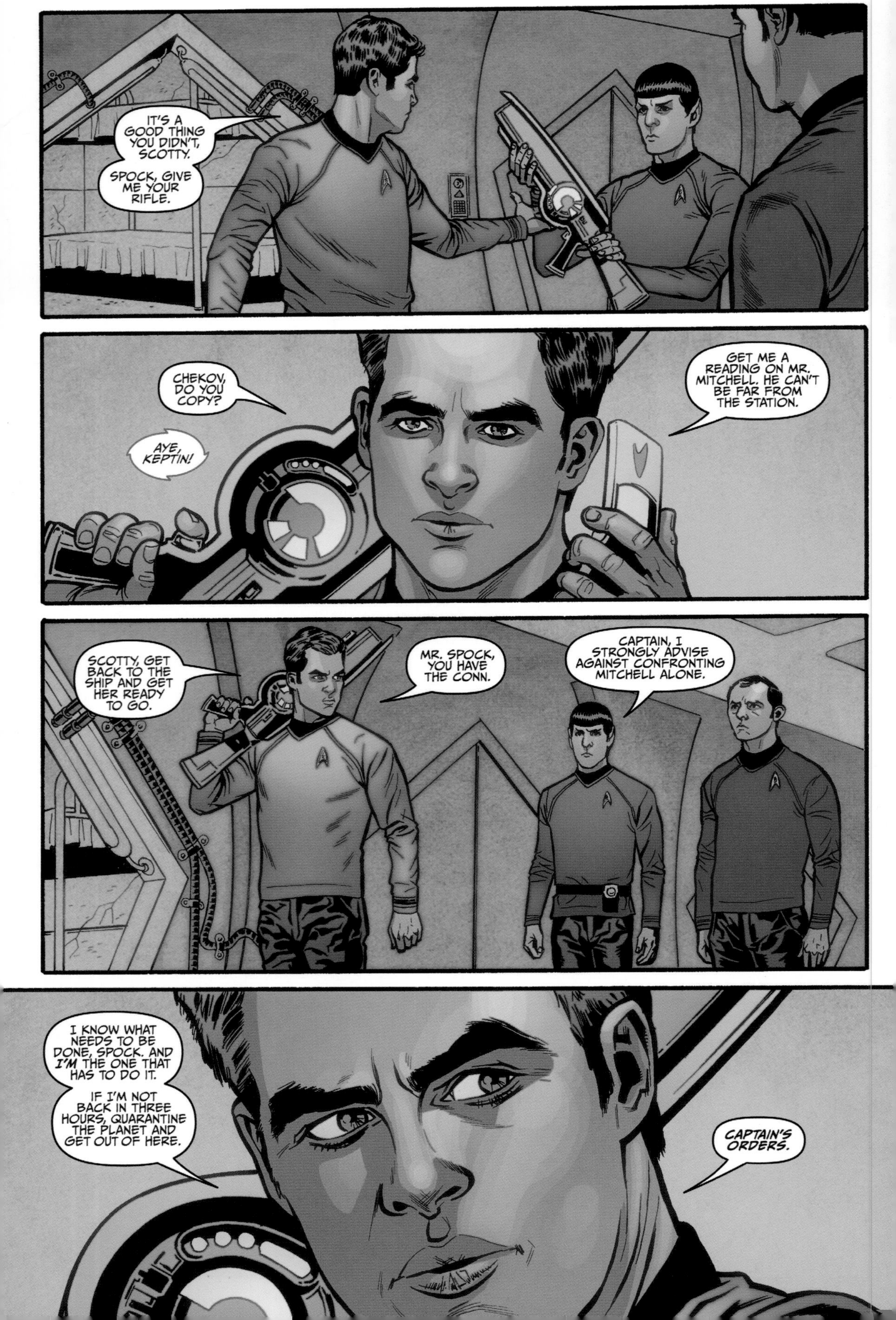
IT'S A GOOD THING YOU DIDN'T, SCOTTY.
SPOCK, GIVE ME YOUR RIFLE.
CHEKOV, DO YOU COPY?
AYE, KEPTIN!
GET ME A READING ON MR. MITCHELL. HE CAN'T BE FAR FROM THE STATION.
SCOTTY, GET BACK TO THE SHIP AND GET HER READY TO GO.
MR. SPOCK, YOU HAVE THE CONN.
CAPTAIN, I STRONGLY ADVISE AGAINST CONFRONTING MITCHELL ALONE.
I KNOW WHAT NEEDS TO BE DONE, SPOCK. AND I'M THE ONE THAT HAS TO DO IT.
IF I'M NOT BACK IN THREE HOURS, QUARANTINE THE PLANET AND GET OUT OF HERE.
CAPTAIN'S ORDERS.

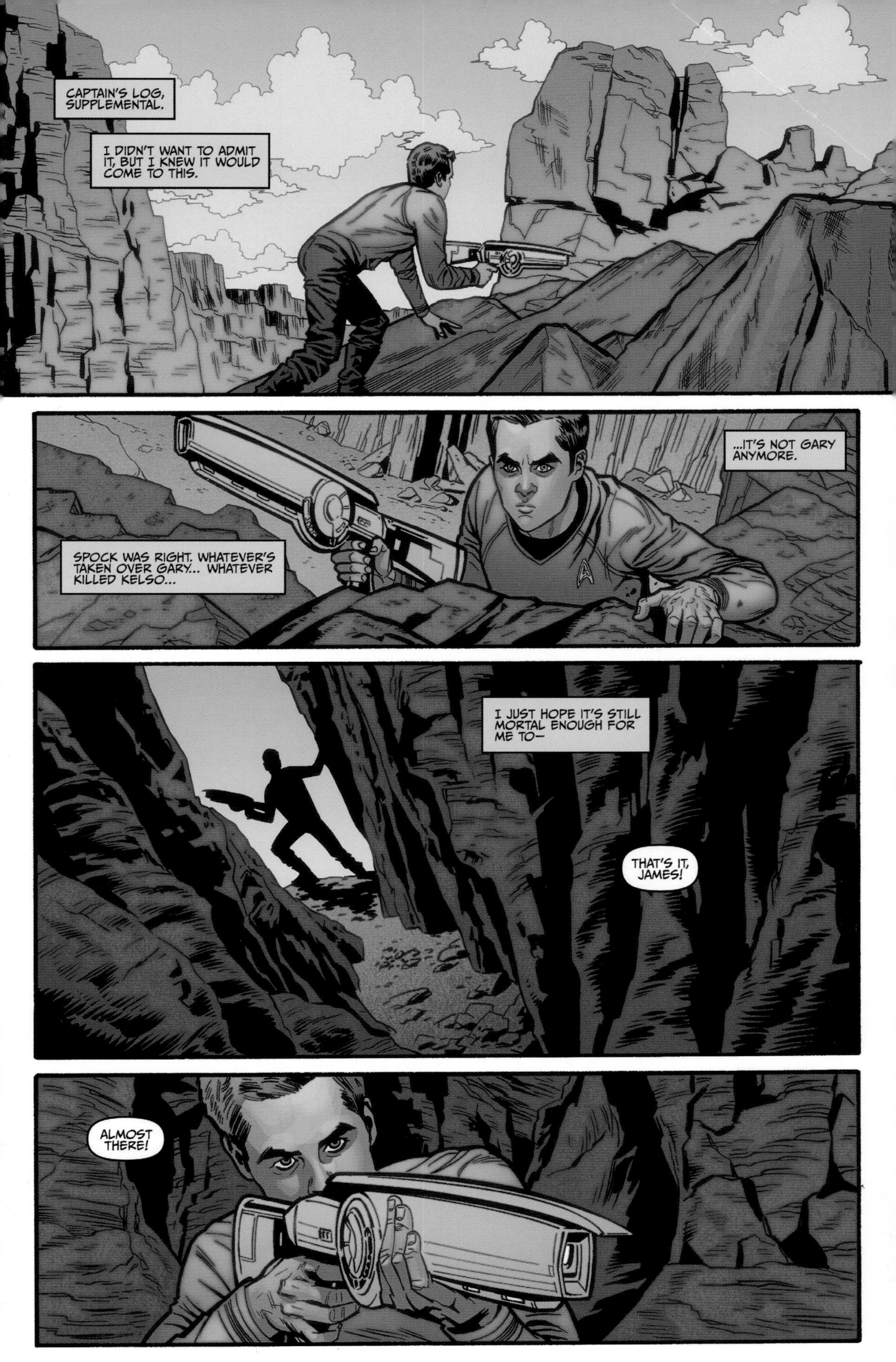
CAPTAIN'S LOG, SUPPLEMENTAL.
I DIDN'T WANT TO ADMIT IT, BUT I KNEW IT WOULD COME TO THIS.
SPOCK WAS RIGHT. WHATEVER'S TAKEN OVER GARY... WHATEVER KILLED KELSO...
...IT'S NOT GARY ANYMORE.
I JUST HOPE IT'S STILL MORTAL ENOUGH FOR ME TO—
THAT'S IT, JAMES!
ALMOST THERE!

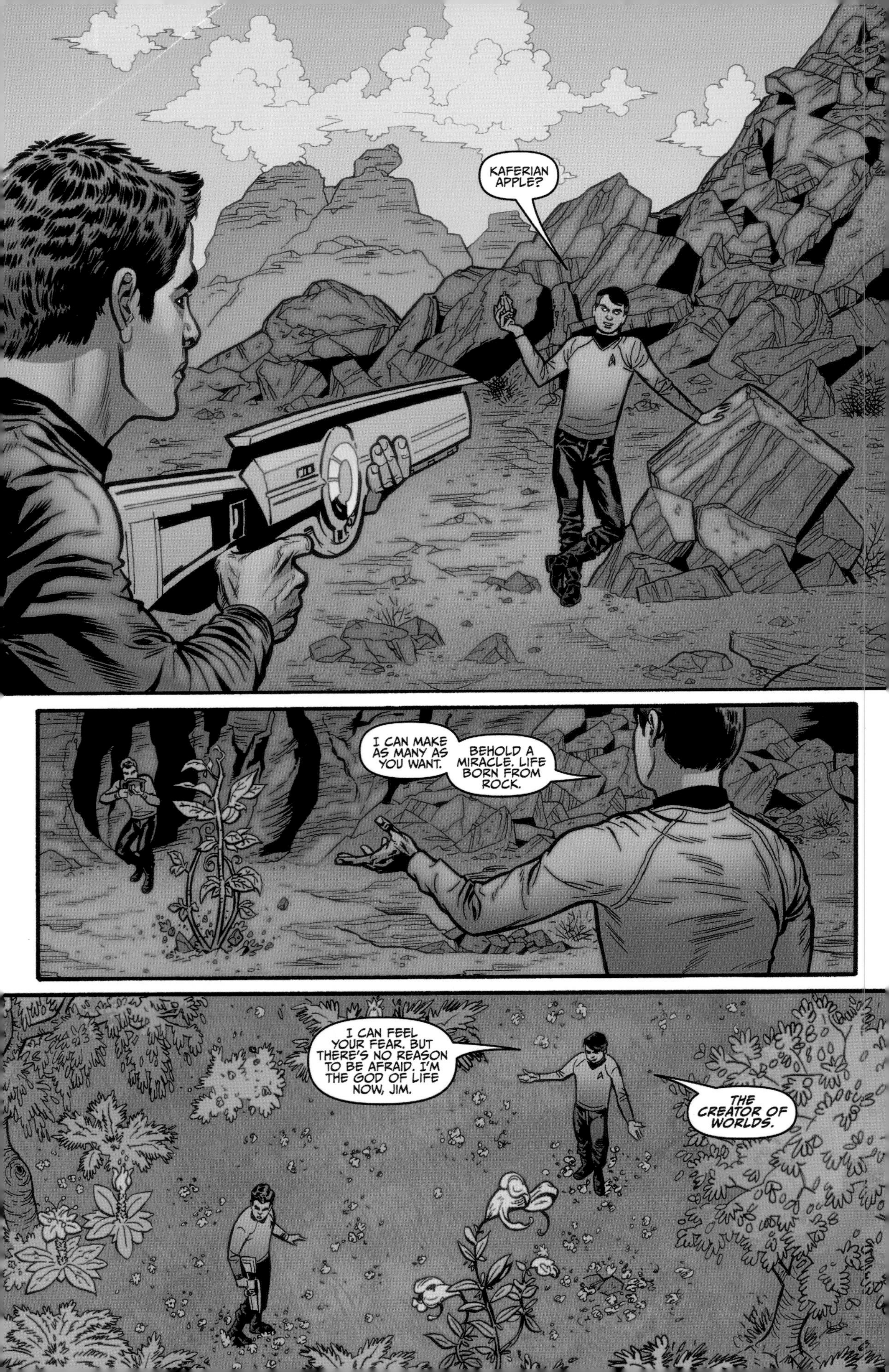
KAFERIAN APPLE?
I CAN MAKE AS MANY AS YOU WANT.
BEHOLD A MIRACLE. LIFE BORN FROM ROCK.
I CAN FEEL YOUR FEAR. BUT THERE'S NO REASON TO BE AFRAID. I'M THE GOD OF LIFE NOW, JIM.
THE CREATOR OF WORLDS.

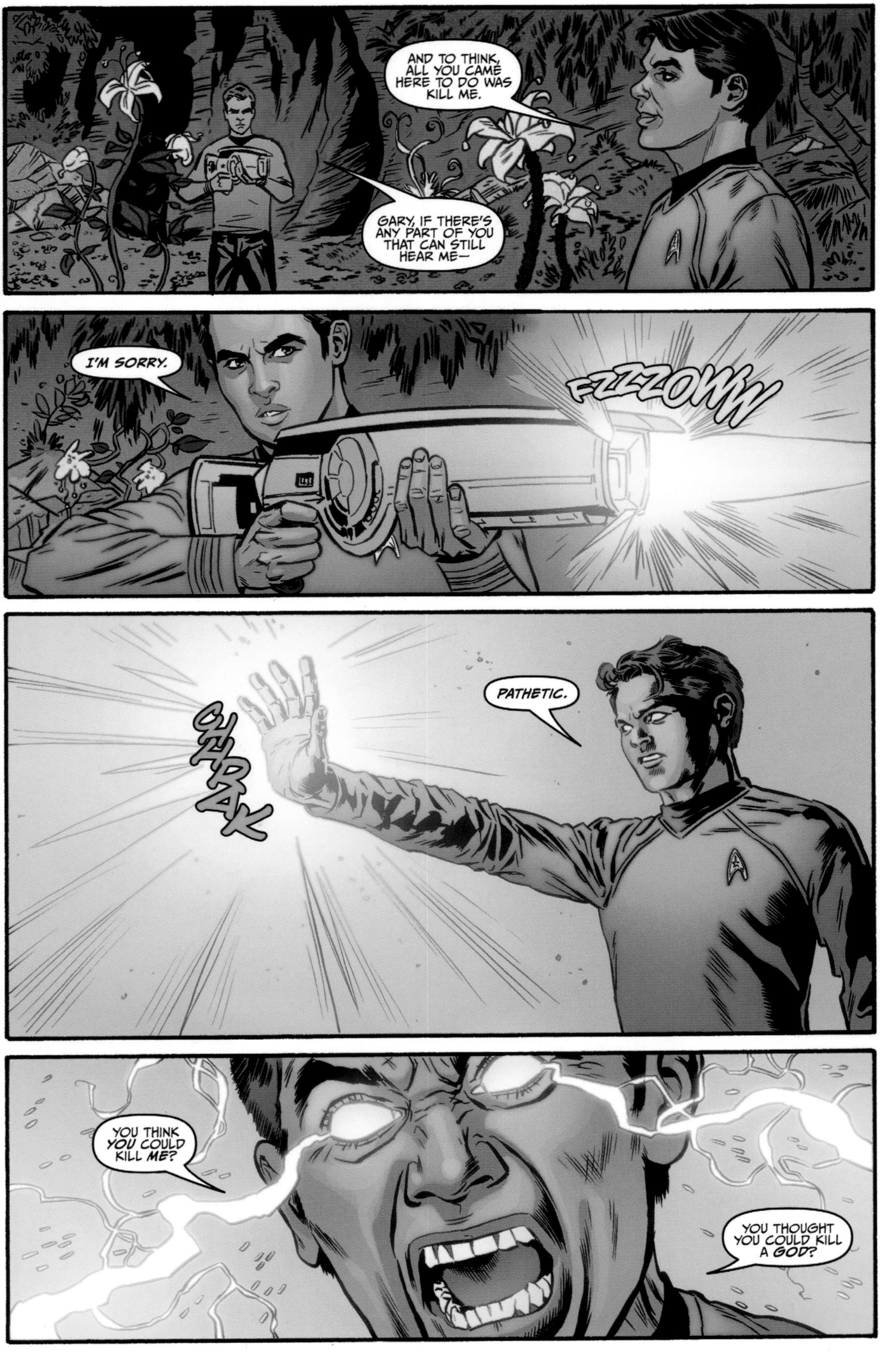

AND TO THINK, ALL YOU CAME HERE TO DO WAS KILL ME.
GARY, IF THERE'S ANY PART OF YOU THAT CAN STILL HEAR ME—
I'M SORRY.
FZZZOWW
CHRAK
PATHETIC.
YOU THINK *YOU* COULD KILL *ME*?
YOU THOUGHT YOU COULD KILL A *GOD*?

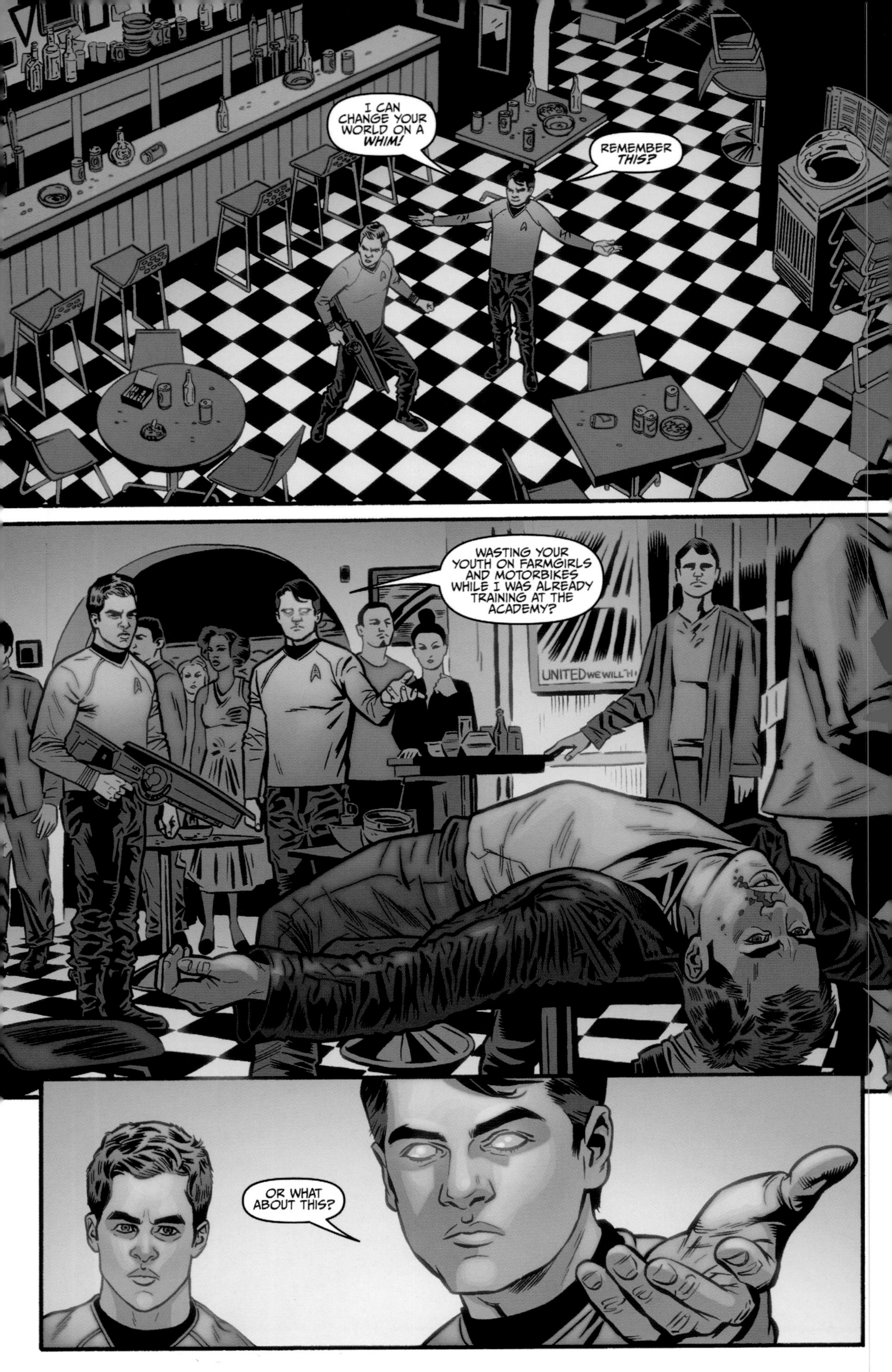
I CAN CHANGE YOUR WORLD ON A *WHIM!*
REMEMBER *THIS?*
WASTING YOUR YOUTH ON FARMGIRLS AND MOTORBIKES WHILE I WAS ALREADY TRAINING AT THE ACADEMY?
UNITED WE WILL
OR WHAT ABOUT THIS?

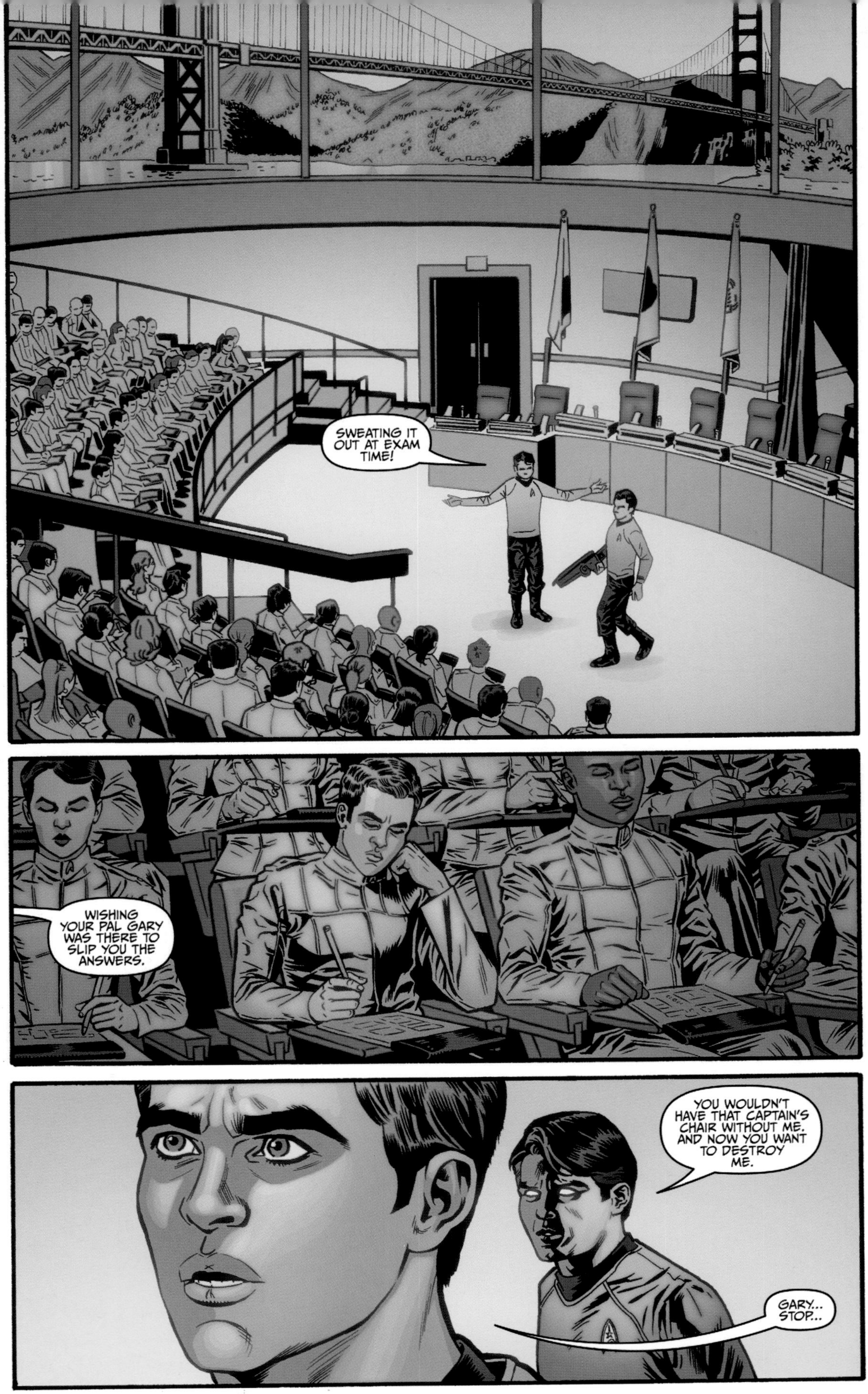
SWEATING IT OUT AT EXAM TIME!
WISHING YOUR PAL GARY WAS THERE TO SLIP YOU THE ANSWERS.
YOU WOULDN'T HAVE THAT CAPTAIN'S CHAIR WITHOUT ME. AND NOW YOU WANT TO DESTROY ME.
GARY... STOP...

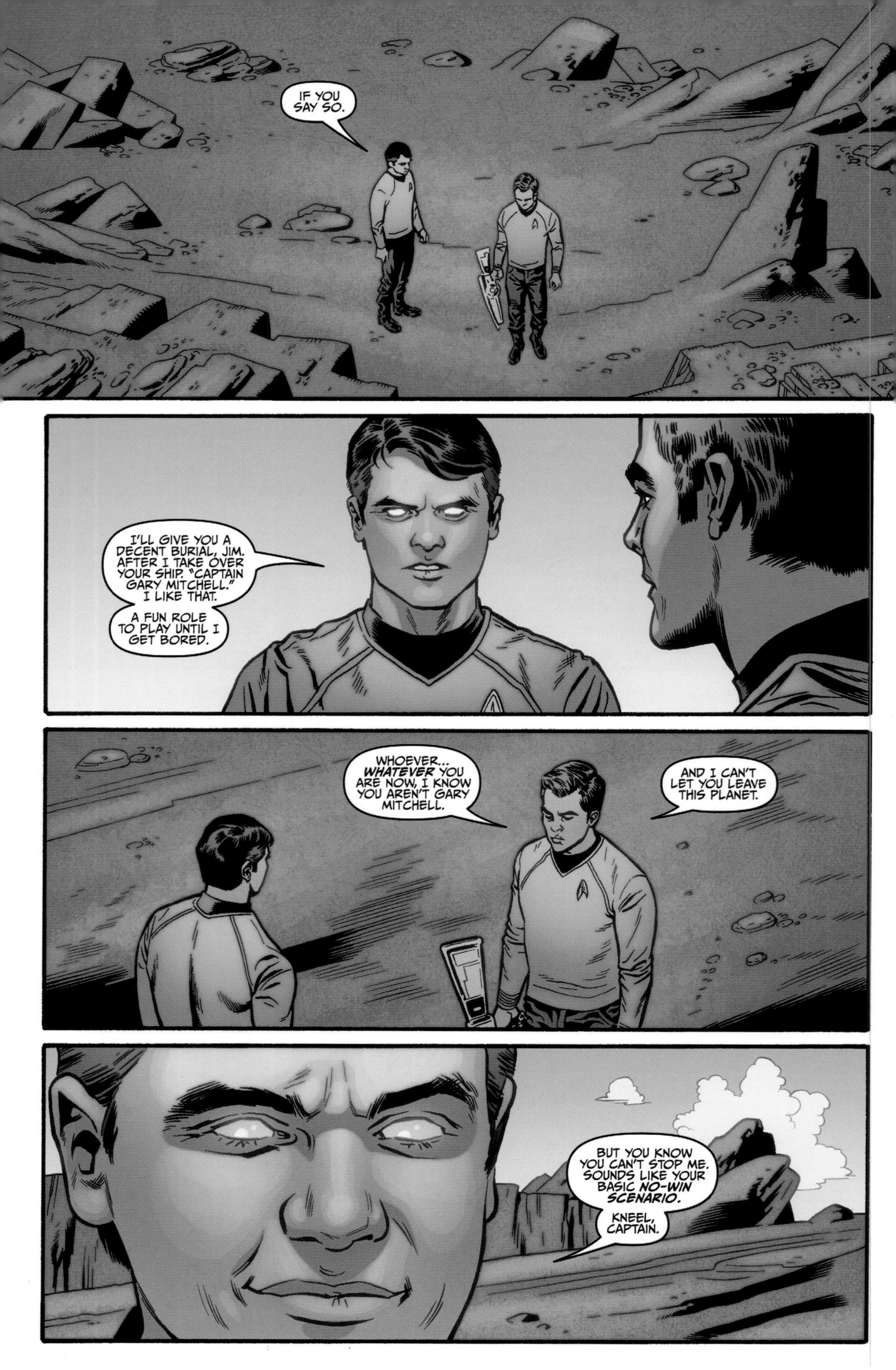
IF YOU SAY SO.
I'LL GIVE YOU A DECENT BURIAL, JIM. AFTER I TAKE OVER YOUR SHIP. "CAPTAIN GARY MITCHELL." I LIKE THAT.
A FUN ROLE TO PLAY UNTIL I GET BORED.
WHOEVER... *WHATEVER* YOU ARE NOW, I KNOW YOU AREN'T GARY MITCHELL.
AND I CAN'T LET YOU LEAVE THIS PLANET.
BUT YOU KNOW YOU CAN'T STOP ME. SOUNDS LIKE YOUR BASIC *NO-WIN SCENARIO.*
KNEEL, CAPTAIN.

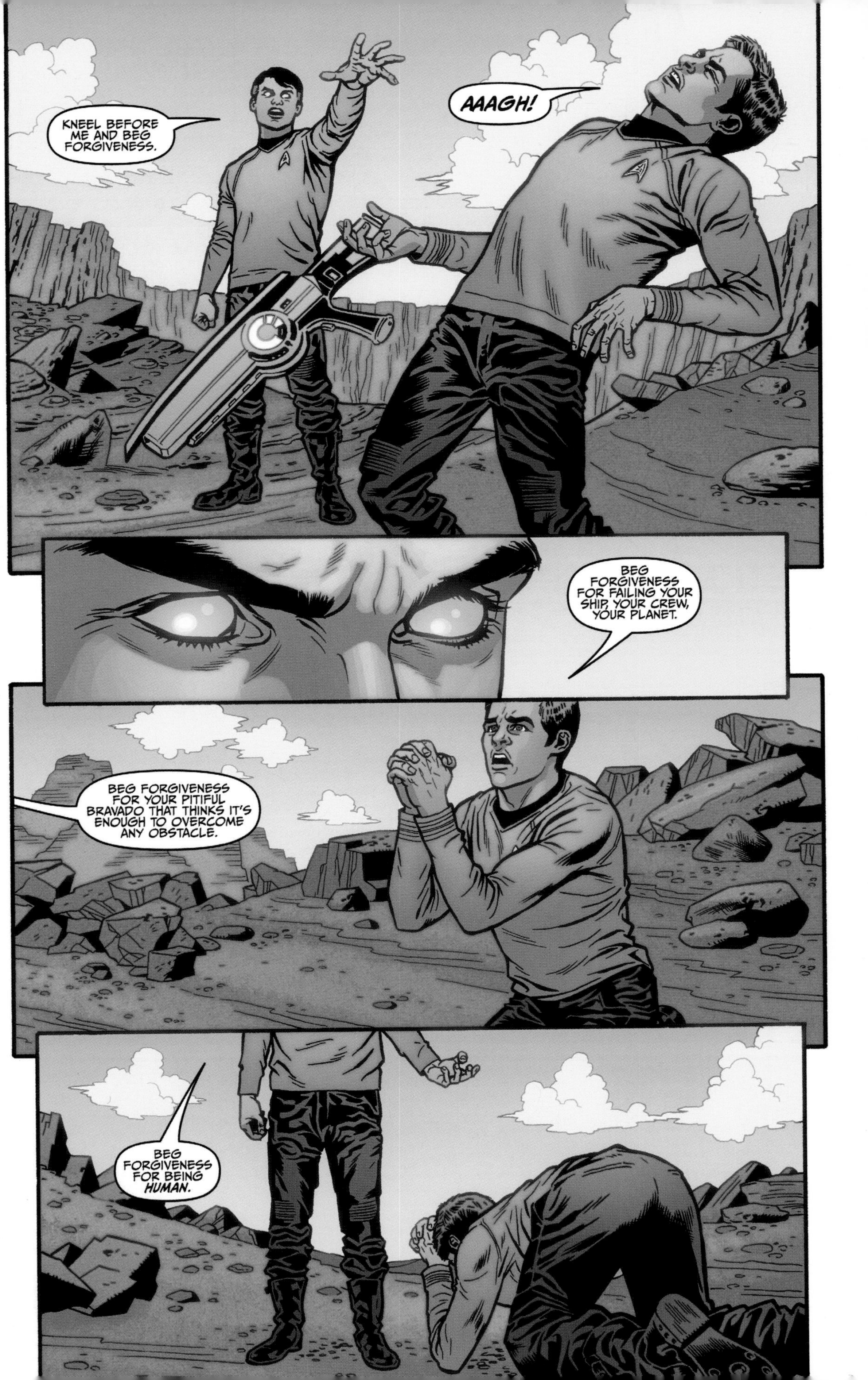
KNEEL BEFORE ME AND BEG FORGIVENESS.
AAAGH!
BEG FORGIVENESS FOR FAILING YOUR SHIP, YOUR CREW, YOUR PLANET.
BEG FORGIVENESS FOR YOUR PITIFUL BRAVADO THAT THINKS IT'S ENOUGH TO OVERCOME ANY OBSTACLE.
BEG FORGIVENESS FOR BEING *HUMAN*.

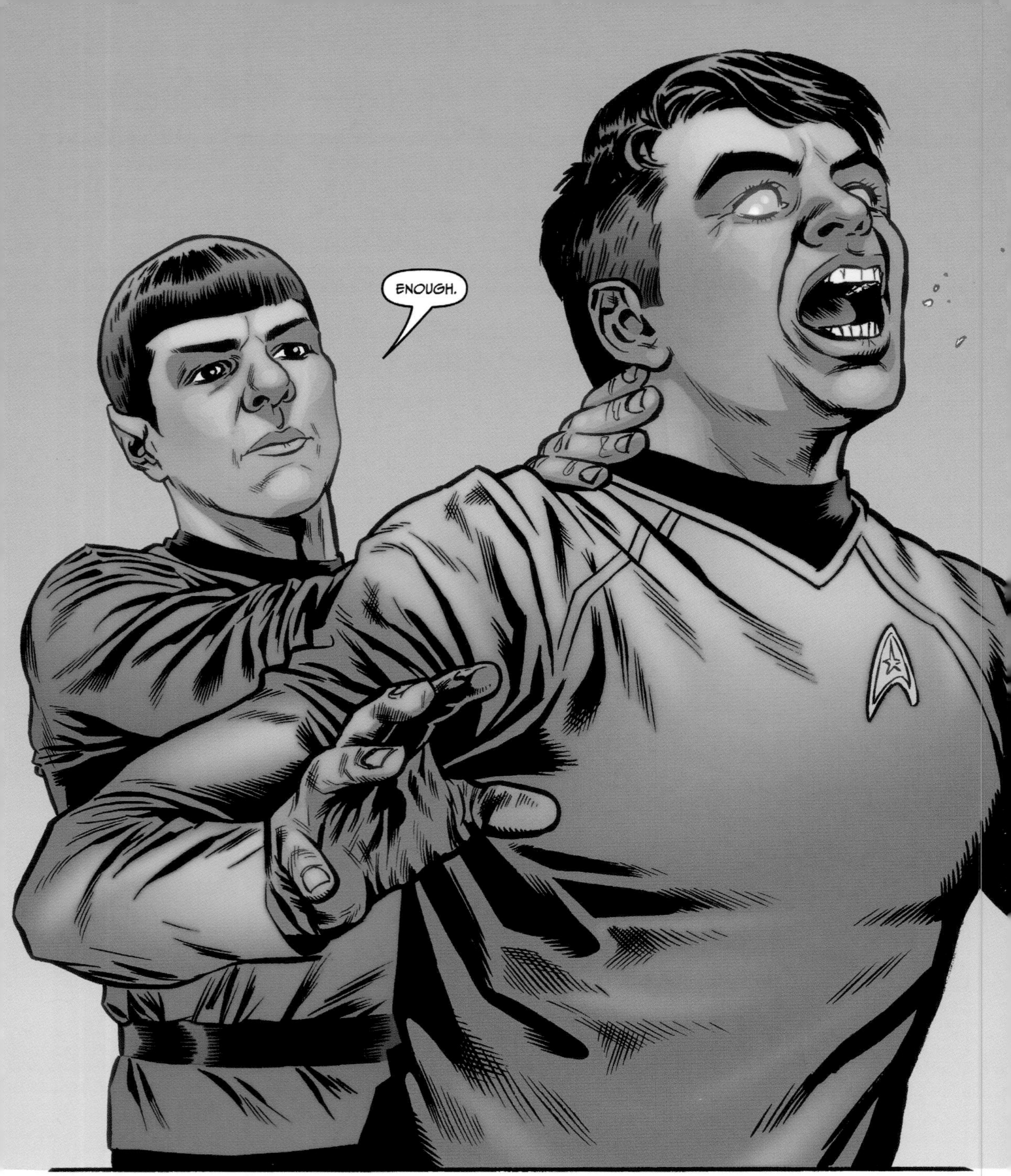
ENOUGH.

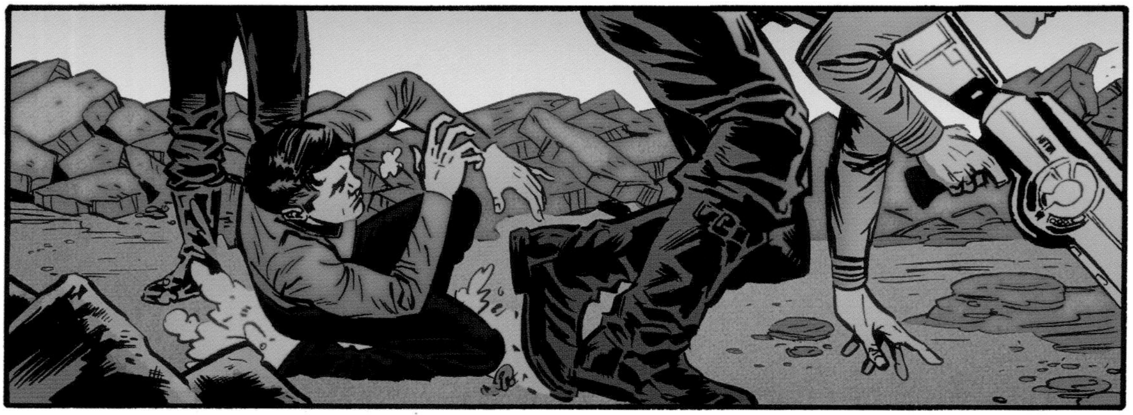

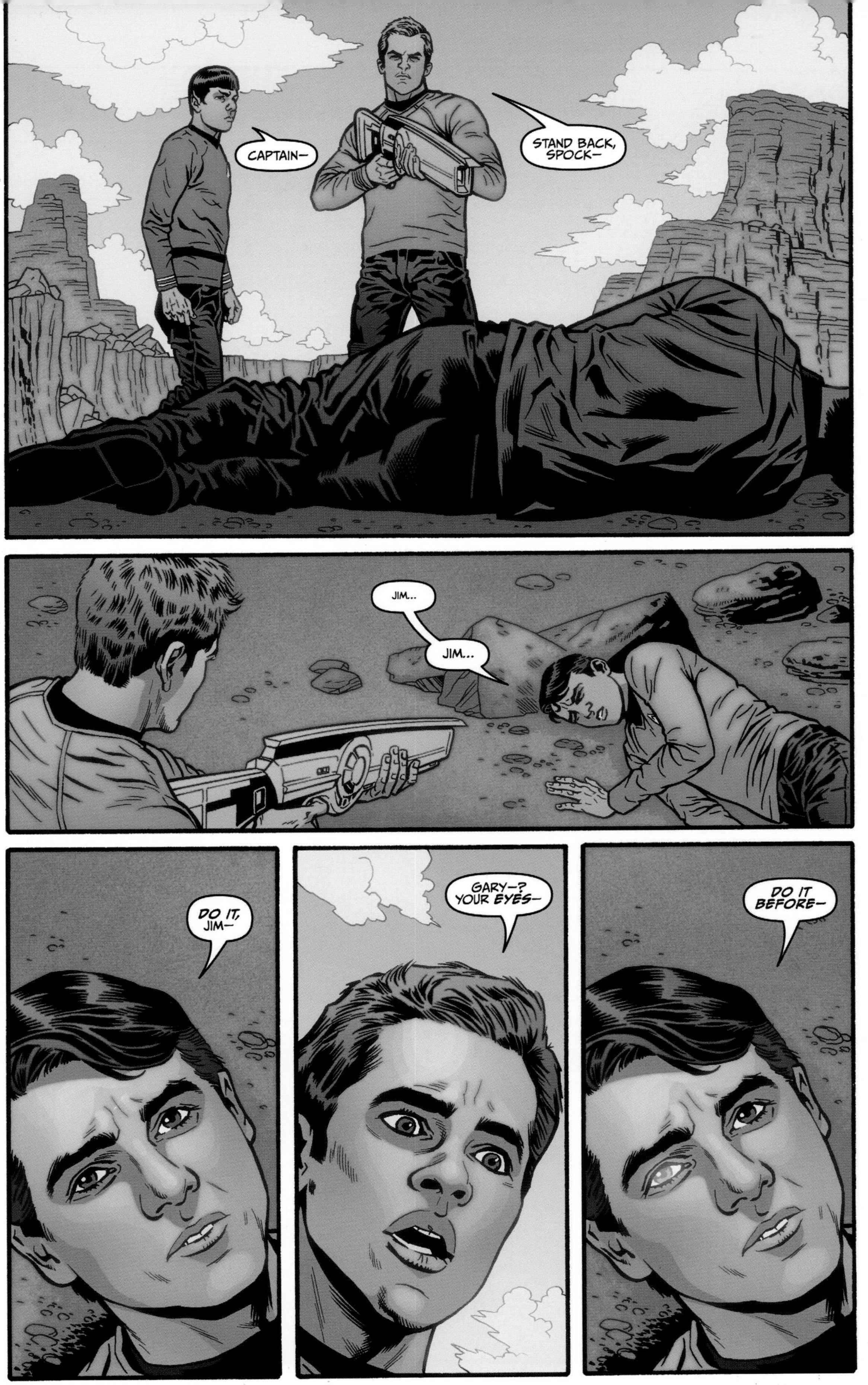
CAPTAIN—
STAND BACK, SPOCK—
JIM...
JIM...
DO IT, JIM—
GARY—? YOUR EYES—
DO IT BEFORE—

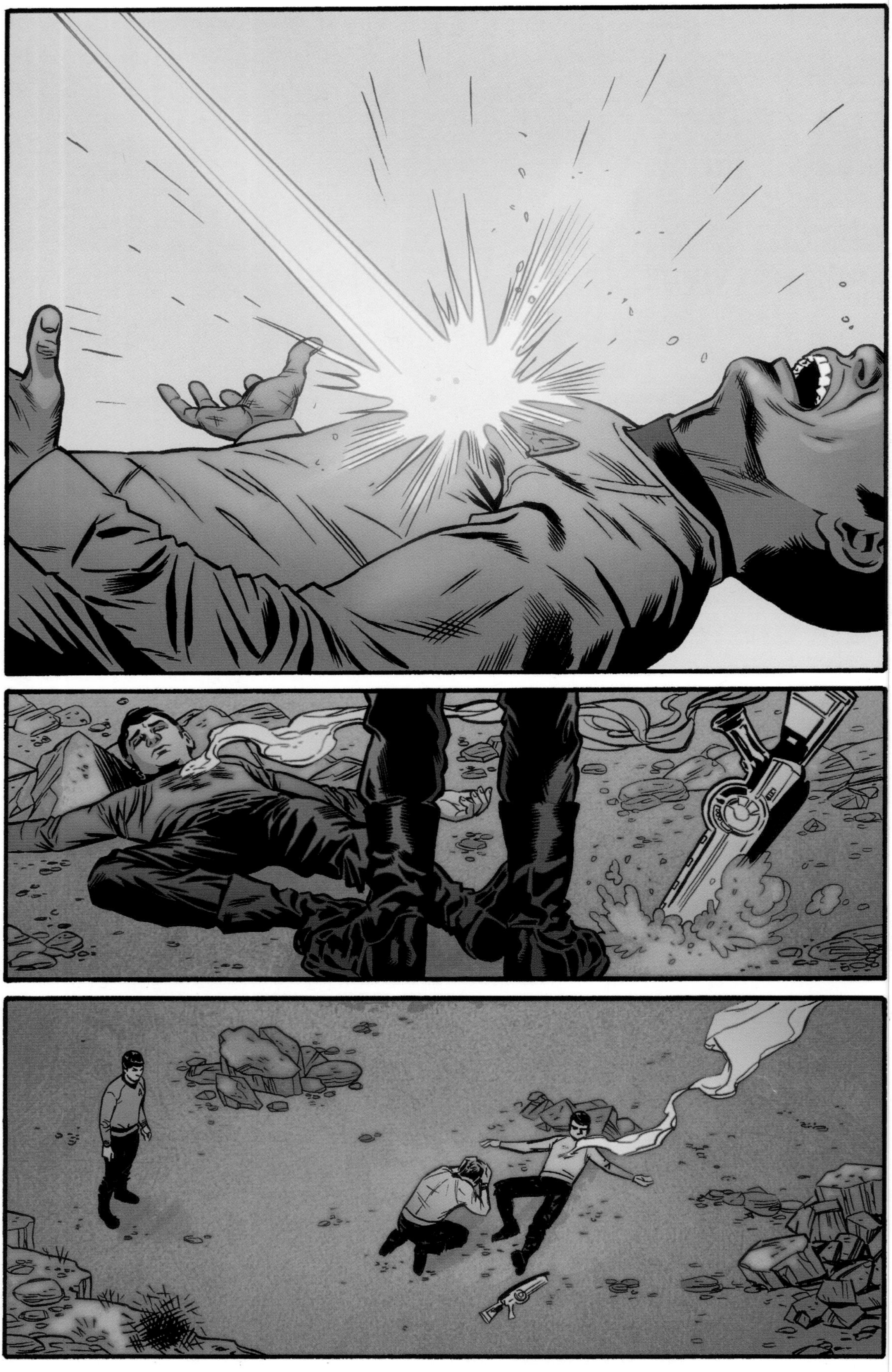

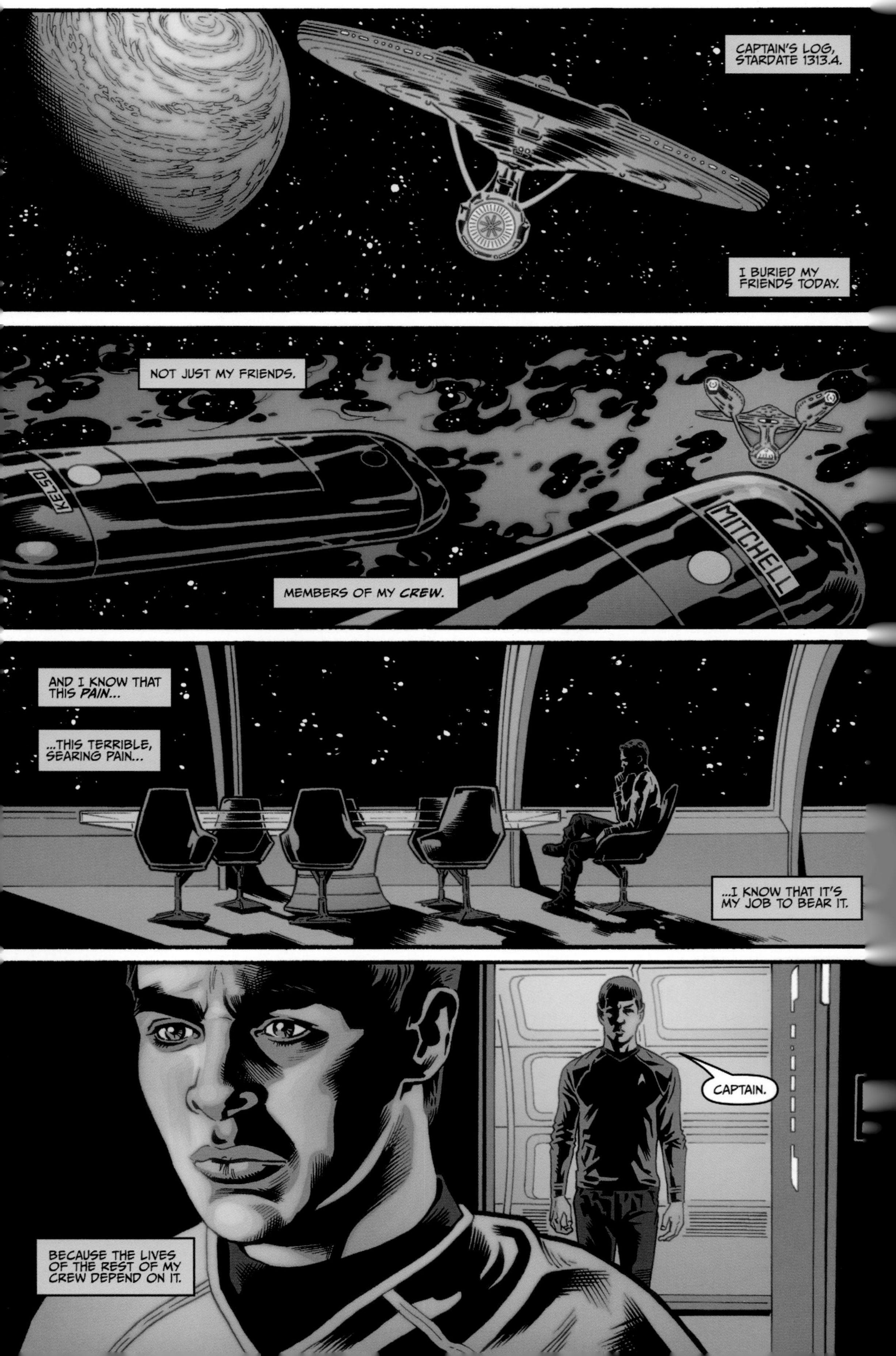
CAPTAIN'S LOG, STARDATE 1313.4.
I BURIED MY FRIENDS TODAY.
NOT JUST MY FRIENDS.
KELSO
MITCHELL
MEMBERS OF MY CREW.
AND I KNOW THAT THIS PAIN...
...THIS TERRIBLE, SEARING PAIN...
...I KNOW THAT IT'S MY JOB TO BEAR IT.
CAPTAIN.
BECAUSE THE LIVES OF THE REST OF MY CREW DEPEND ON IT.

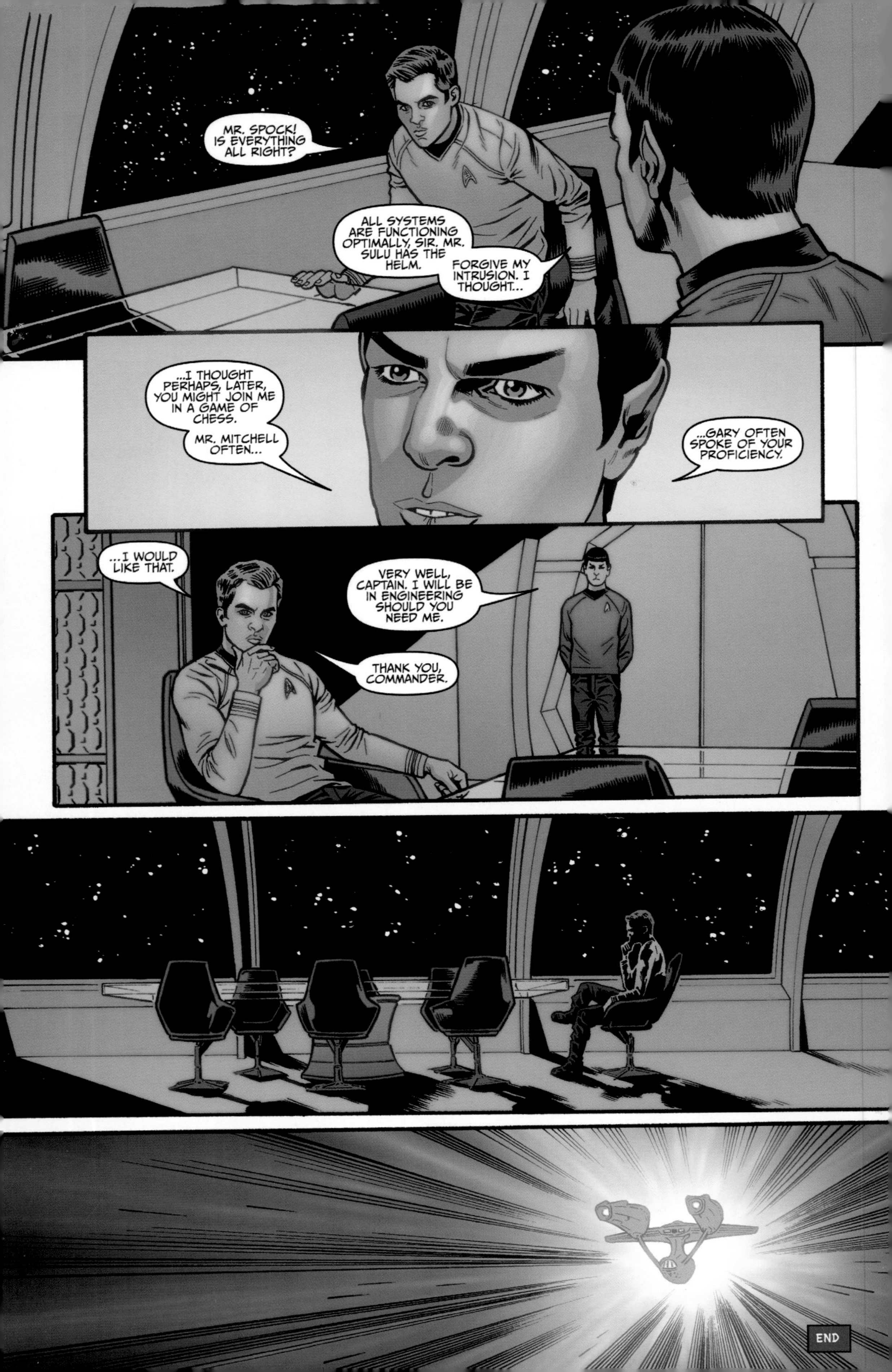
MR. SPOCK! IS EVERYTHING ALL RIGHT?
ALL SYSTEMS ARE FUNCTIONING OPTIMALLY, SIR. MR. SULU HAS THE HELM.
FORGIVE MY INTRUSION. I THOUGHT...
...I THOUGHT PERHAPS, LATER, YOU MIGHT JOIN ME IN A GAME OF CHESS.
MR. MITCHELL OFTEN...
...GARY OFTEN SPOKE OF YOUR PROFICIENCY.
...I WOULD LIKE THAT.
VERY WELL, CAPTAIN. I WILL BE IN ENGINEERING SHOULD YOU NEED ME.
THANK YOU, COMMANDER.
END